THE

BARBER

Also by Kelly Barker

Novels

The Inner Temple

Even the Gods Fear It

Necromantia

THE BARBER

By Kelly Barker

Printed and bound in Great Britain by Amazon 2023

Dedicated to all barbers.

The Barber

The new neighbours, who moved in only a couple of months back, were now called the bloody neighbours from forty-six. Katie, a newcomer herself, was standing at the end of her drive with the two women who lived on either side of her, discussing them.

"Didn't you hear her shouting at him? It was going on for ages," Sarah said to Katie.

Before she could answer, Rosy said, "And she was hitting, kicking and spitting on him. When he locked himself in his car to get away from her, she started kicking it. In the end, I called out from my window, asking him if he wanted me to call the police. It soon stopped after that—"

"It didn't," Sarah interrupted. "I could still hear them shouting when they went back inside their house."

Apparently, *the bloody neighbours from forty-six* had come home from a bender at three in the morning, and were arguing about something or other, before the girlfriend went *Mike Tyson* on her boyfriend.

"I didn't hear a thing," Katie said. Which surprised her, considering she wasn't sleeping well. Something strange was happening, which prompted her to look into sleep paralysis. The article she'd read said it was common, but not common if it happens frequently. The article mentioned nothing about a man standing over you while you slept.

"You must sleep like the dead then,"—Sarah pointed at her, then to all the houses within the Cul-de-sac—"because you're the only one that didn't hear them."

"Nope, not a peep. And I haven't been sleeping like the dead either. Do you two know anything about sleep paralysis?"

They both looked taken aback by the abrupt change of subject before Rosy said, "It happened to me a few years back. It's scary because you can't move or scream. I thought I was going to have a heart attack."

Pleased that she wasn't the only one, she asked, "Was someone standing over you when it happened?"

"Oh, no." She shook her head. "Why do you ask?"

Even though Katie was new to Hailey Road, she felt at ease around Sarah and Rosy. They were easygoing and open-minded, so she spoke freely.

"Every time it happens to me, I see a man in white standing in the corner of my bedroom." She rubbed her hands down her face. "But this morning, he was standing beside my bed, over me."

It sounded ridiculous, saying it aloud, and she waited for them to make fun of her. But they both just looked at each other, then at nothing in particular.

Sarah cleared her throat. "Did you read the story in the news about the couple who lived in your house before you? The couple who wanted to remain anonymous?"

"Not that anyone could remain anonymous around here," Rosy said.

Katie shook her head. "What story?"

"They said their house was haunted, and the husband said he woke up to a ghost trying to cut his hair." At that, they all giggled. Who wouldn't?

"Really? My house?" Katie didn't believe in that rubbish. We lived in a day and age, where all myths were now proven to be a hoax or scientifically explained. Even the sleep demon myth was now known as sleep paralysis. Although, she wouldn't have known that had she not experienced it herself lately.

"They really believed it, too. The house was back on the market shortly after they moved in."

Before Katie bought the house, she'd brazenly offered ten-thousand below the asking price. A price that was already below the market value. She'd been beyond shocked when the owners accepted her offer on the same day, and now she knew why.

3

"How about the people who lived there before the couple?"

Rosy tilted her head to the side. "They weren't there long either, come to think of it. No mention of a ghost, though." She smiled.

Katie returned her smile. "And you won't hear me mention anything about ghosts either. Just weird nightmares about a man in white."

When she thought the subject was about to change to something a little lighter, Sarah asked her to describe the man's white attire.

"Oh, umm. It's just the top half that's white. I think his trousers are black. Although, I'm not entirely certain because I can't move my head to see, and when I'm no longer paralysed, he's gone and everything goes back to normal."

"Except your pounding heart," Rosy added.

"True."

"Describe the top to me," Sarah repeated her odd question.

"I don't know." She shrugged. "It's like what a doctor would have worn back in the day. Oh, I know. It's like a tunic, something a beautician or a dentist would wear."

"Like something a barber would have worn back in the day?"

"Yes, that's right. Now that you've said it, he definitely looks like an old-school barber. He even had a comb in his front pocket."

"Oooh, looks like the previous neighbours weren't completely bananas after all." Rosy said, then clapped her hands together. "Anyway, I have to get back to work. Would you grab me some rum-and-raisin ice cream when you go to Lidl?"

"It's already on my list," Sarah said.

"And you should wear a hat in bed from now on. You wouldn't want to wake up to a buzz cut."

Katie laughed, then sobered when she noticed that Sarah barely cracked a smile. Curiosity got the best of her, so after they said their goodbyes, she stepped in front of Sarah. "Tell me more about what the previous couple said."

"Katie, don't worry about it. It's probably just a coincidence."

"What's a coincidence? Tell me. I don't believe in all that ghost rubbish, anyway."

Sarah took a moment before answering. "Years ago, before my time, a barber lived and worked in your house. If you look there,"—she pointed above her window—"you'll see some bricks are more faded than the others. That's where his sign was."

Katie looked. "I hadn't noticed that before. Maybe that's where the couple got their story from."

"Possibly. But you didn't know about the barber, did you? So that doesn't explain where you got your story from, does it?"

Apple Tree

Willow pushed Malcolm's hand away again when he reached out. "This is taking longer than expected," she said to herself. Her brows furrowed. "I'll be back in a moment, darling."

"Will... ow," he rasped. "Need a doctor."

"My darling husband, you don't need a doctor." She ran the backs of her fingers along his jaw. "What you need is in the garden."

She stood, put the chair back in the room's corner, then glanced in the mirror so she could see herself to straighten her long, black dress. Her hand was on the door handle when she remembered something. "Oh, I almost forgot." She walked over to the bed where her husband lay and collected the bowl from the bedside table. "I know how important it is to you that everything be put back in its place after its been used. I'll bring you more soup."

"No... Please, I need..."

"I won't be long." She opened the bedroom door and walked down the stairs to their spotless kitchen—which was not at all like this when her great grandma was alive. The corners of Willow's lips curled when she pictured how it once was: herbs hanging from the rack, flour scattered over the worktop and floor, a pantry filled with jars of jam and beetroot, an apple pie cooling on the chopping board, and there was always something bubbling away on the stove. If she concentrated, she could smell the aromas from the past. Her half smile faded. "I miss you, Grandma."

Today, of all days, she needed to feel her grandma's presence, and now there was only one place left where she felt it: the apple tree in the back garden. She put the bowl on the worktop with no intention of washing it up, took a basket from the cupboard, then made her way to the back door. The day was glorious for late October; it could easily be mistaken for spring if it were not for the fallen leaves scattered in the grass. Before she made her way to the tree, she looked over to the left at her vegetable patch, making a note of what she needed to relieve her husband's pain, which was planted between the carrots and Brussels sprouts.

The apple tree she sought was magnificent: not only did it tower above all others, it also possessed the strength to hold on to all its leaves throughout winter. Willow could almost hear her grandma's voice as she approached it. They had spent so much time underneath it, come wind, rain or shine. She collected a couple of fallen apples off the roots that protruded from the ground, then took a seat on one, next to the tiny mushrooms that sprung from the damp bark. "Oh, Grandma, I tried to follow your recipe, but he is still struggling to breathe. It's been three weeks now." She threw an apple into the gooseberry bush.

When her grandma died, Willow had inherited the house. It was Victorian, with bay windows at the front, an outside toilet, and no central heating; not that they needed it. The fire kept the house warm during the night and the thousands of books that lined the walls retained the heat during the day. She sighed. If Malcolm had not thrown her grandma's books away, she'd know how best to help him. Against her will, her thoughts returned to that day.

"This house needs modernising," he had said, shortly after their wedding. He had stripped the house back to bricks and mortar, painted it grey and white, replaced the wicker chairs for a corner sofa, and replaced the oak table for a glass one. Willow had hated the thought of it, but only agreed to the renovation because Malcom had promised her he would build her a bigger bookcase, but he never did. He had said that the builders had thrown all her books in the skip by mistake, and therefore, she no longer needed one.

"The books wouldn't have gone with the new interior. Why can't you understand that? Look at how much nicer it looks without that clutter," he had said sharply, while she wept. "You should be grateful I took the time and had the money to make this house livable."

Willow had regrettably argued that it was actually her money that had paid for this so-called 'higher standard of living'. She threw another apple into the gooseberry bush. Some of those books had recipes within them that her great, great grandmother and grandma had handwritten. The only recipes she could now remember were the ones her grandma had taught her under this tree. Her thought returned to the time they were cutting apples into quarters.

"Now, remember, we need exactly two hundred and one apple seeds," her grandma had said.

"Why two hundred and one? Why not just two hundred?" the much younger Willow had said.

"The extra one is for luck, my sweet girl."

"And what are we making?" she asked, while popping three more seeds into the jar.

"We're going to make a special pie for your grandad. He's been very angry lately, and this will cheer him up and then keep him quiet."

Willow looked up at her grandma's bruised eye. "Why has Grandad been angry with you?"

"It's the drink; it makes him do stupid things," was all she had said.

After her grandad died, the house had become a haven—no more shouting, slamming furniture around, and no more hitting and hair-pulling. She and her grandma had found peace; not that she had known any differently until then. Thank goodness her husband was nothing like her grandad. It had pleased her to learn that Malcom never drank a single drop. He said he didn't like to feel out of control—something Willow now more than understood.

Her husband was a doctor, and they had met shortly after her grandma died, when she'd fallen into a deep depression. He'd told her she was still grieving and perhaps felt lonely, and had said that all she needed was someone to talk to—he was right. He had made several calls to see how she was getting on with the grievance counsellor before he suggested they meet for a coffee. She smiled to herself when she remembered the phone call and how he had so confidently asked—no, not asked—suggested. Her heart had instantly lifted; there was a light at the end of her gloomy tunnel, and they had fallen in love almost immediately. He had been so impressed with her house when she first invited him over for dinner. "A house like this must be worth a fortune," he had said.

Three months after their first coffee date, he had taken her to Rome and asked her to marry him; another three months after that, they were married. Everything had happened so fast and it felt like he had yanked the rug from beneath her feet. But wasn't that what love was: to feel swept off your feet?

Willow plucked a few mushrooms from the apple tree's roots, then popped them into her basket. The mushrooms were called *amanita phalloides,* also known as death cap mushrooms. She was proud of herself for remembering what they were called when other memories came to mind. Her grandma had been so knowledgeable about plants and would spend hours telling Willow what they were called, where they were from, and their various uses.

She had told her about the legends that accompanied them too: how the Norse Berserker warriors had taken *aconite* (wolfbane) to shapeshift into wolves before battle, or how witches would rub *belladonna* (deadly nightshade) into their thighs to enable them to fly on their broomsticks. Her grandma had also taught her that everything Mother Nature created had a purpose and how important it was to give

11

back what we took. Willow had never fully understood the meaning of that until she helped bury her grandad under the bramble bush. The blackberries had been divine and plentiful the following year.

Now, there was one more thing she needed to help her poor husband: *hemlock.* As she was about to stand, she noticed a black toad resting on her dress. "Hello, little one. It's too cold for you to be out now," she said, cupping the toad in her hand and placing it in the basket.

On the way back to the house, she stopped at her vegetable patch. The *hemlock* had wilted, but that mattered very little; it was the roots she needed. Willow kneeled in the soil, not caring that her dress was now dirty, and used her fingers like a rake to loosen the soil, then started pulling out of the ground what looked like skinny parsnips. She pulled up as many as she could find this time. *Too many is better than too few*, she thought. Then she carefully lifted the black toad from the basket, placed it in the shallow hole from which the roots had been pulled, and then covered it with loose soil and fallen leaves. "You need to sleep, little one. See you next year."

. . .

While Willow was boiling the *hemlock* roots and mushrooms in a pot, she heard a thump from upstairs—her dear husband must have fallen out of bed again.

"I'm coming, darling," she called out, hoping he'd heard. Bless him, he was in so much pain, but he wouldn't be for much longer. She quickly added salt and pepper to the soup, then poured it into a bowl. She didn't bother with a tray as she made her way out of the kitchen to the stairs.

As she rounded the corner, she jumped back when she saw her husband's hand clawing over the top step. "Oh, darling." She put the soup down and took two steps at a time to reach him.

He was wheezing as he tried to talk.

"It's okay." She brushed his fringe out of his eyes. "I'm here now."

Not knowing any other way to get him back into the bedroom, she grabbed him by the ankles and dragged him while he was on his stomach. He tried in vain to hold on to the top step, but he was too drained. Once they were inside, she knew it would be impossible to lift him onto the bed, so she grabbed his pillow, put it beside his head, then rolled him over.

"Willow... please." He tried to reach out to her.

"I'll be right back. My soup will ease your pain, I promise." She rushed out of the room, then came back again with the bowl.

"No, Willow... please."

She put the soup on the side table and took another pillow from the bed. Malcolm flinched when she brought it over his face. She looked from him to the pillow, frowned, then looked back at him. "Don't be silly," she chided. "I just need to prop your head up a little so I can feed you."

She gently lifted his head and lowered it onto the pillow, then kneeled beside him with the soup. When he tried to push her away with his feeble attempts, he spilt soup from the bowl. "Malcolm, we can either do this the easy way or the hard way. Don't make me sit on you."

"Why, Willow? Why?"

"Because you wanted to cut my grandma's apple tree down, that's why. Now, open your mouth."

. . .

One year later.

Willow sat under the tree with one of her new books and her lunch—she had made herself an apple and cinnamon pie. The apples from her tree had been perfect this year; full-flavoured, brightly coloured, and bigger than any other year she could remember. She looked over her shoulder at the loose soil between the roots of the tree. Her grandma was right; to fully reap Mother Nature's gifts, you must give back what you take.

ABOUT THE AUTHOR

Kelly Barker was born in Oxford and now lives in Witney with her husband and dog, Lana. She has been a barber for over twenty years, and loves her job, however, reading and writing is her true passion—a passion handed down to her from her great grandmother, Isobel O'Leary.

www.kellybarker.org

THE
INNER
TEMPLE

SLEEP-DEPRIVED WRITER SOON BECOMES
LOST IN THE WORLD SHE CREATED...

KELLY BARKER

Sleep-deprived Zoe lives in her own imagination, struggling between home and work life as a barber... finding it easier each day to slip into a world that doesn't exist. Or does it?

Hell bent on completing a story she is writing to right a wrong, she unknowingly creates a storyline so powerful, it gives the main character Ivy—a vampire queen—the means to escape off the pages and into the real world.

To secure her freedom, Ivy must destroy the writer. However, Zoe doesn't know what's real or what her mind has conjured. Is this a part of her overactive imagination? Or can she accept her gift, using it to send Ivy back within the pages?

Zoe is torn between her newfound abilities to create characters into existence through her storytelling and her loved ones. Her fiance Bowen wants to protect her, but she feels as though she can't breathe.

When Bowen sets sail, taking one last trip to save the plesiosaurs from extinction, she and Varik, one of her creations, release something so deadly it's rumoured that even the gods fear it.

She is now faced with two choices. With the world divided over her creations, the line between right and wrong has become blurred. Will Zoe finally understand that you can't have all that power without repercussions? Or will she lose everything?

Cokehead Max comes from a long line of spiritualists. With each generation becoming more powerful than the last to fulfil a prophecy bestowed upon them.

When Max's grandma dies, not only is he forced into a world he wants no part of, he has to pay his grandma's debt for violating the rules governed by Ebony – the guardian of the realm between life and death.

Can Max's family – divided by secrecy and grief – unite to defeat both the prophecy and the seemingly rogue guardian? Or is it too late?

www.kellybarker.org

Printed in Great Britain
by Amazon

25257061R00020